THE UN-TOLD STORY

The Trial
of the
Big Bad Wolf

Liam Farrell

Illustrations: Terry Myler

WANTED

THE CHILDREN'S PRESS

To my son Jeremy,
the original of the species

First published 2002 by
The Children's Press
an imprint of Anvil Books
45 Palmerston Road, Dublin 6

2 4 6 8 7 5 3 1

ISBN 1 901737 40 3

Typeset by Computertype Limited
Printed by Colour Books Limited

Contents

1 My Diary 4

2 *The Daily Howl* 10

3 The Trial Begins 12

4 Grandma Comes a Cropper 20

5 Miss M Turns up Trumps! 28

6 More from *The Daily Howl* 34

7 Dirty Work at the Crossroads 36

8 Uproar in Court! 51

9 *The Daily Howl* Sums Up 59

1 My Diary

When you last heard from me, I was
locked up in a cold damp cell,
awaiting trial. The Three Little Pigs
had accused me of Breaking and
Entering and causing Criminal
Damage to two of their houses.

I only have to re-read my diary to
relive those terrible days.

Day 1: Share with 'Snorer' Polecat.
Don't get a wink of sleep all night.

Day 2: Food – lumpy porridge, sour milk – uneatable. Write to old family solicitors, Frog & Sprog.

Joined by 'Wheezer' Stoat, who wheezes all night, spreading millions of germs. Cover my nose and throat. I nearly suffocate.

Day 3: Porridge burnt to cinders. No word from Frog & Sprog.

Another inmate joins us: 'Croker' Ferret. Four in a cell for two! Write to RIP (Rights in Prison) to complain about cold, damp, food, lack of space.

Day 4: No word from Frog & Sprog.

Day 5: Can't phone them. Calls only allowed one day a month – yesterday.

Outside the cell window I hear the shrill voices of the Three Little Pigs:

In despair, I write to World Wide Wolves@last ditch.com.

Day 6: Croker says, 'You're for it!' He tosses over a copy of *The Daily Howl.*

I'm front page news! Across the top in great big black letters are the words:

TRIAL OF THE BIG BAD WOLF STARTS NEXT WEEK

The warder appears. 'Visitor for you. Your solicitor.'

Had there been room in the cell I would fallen to my knees to thank God. Frog & Sprog had come to the rescue! From now on, I could put myself in the hands of dear old silver-haired Mr Frog.

In the waiting-room, feet on the
table, was a brash young fellow in a
purple suit and a pink satin tie! Hair
glued together in a cock's comb.

'I expected to see Mr Frog *senior*.'

'The da? Conked out last week.'

'He's dead?'

'As a doornail. Stiff. Stretched.
Snuffed. Shafted. Not to worry! Here's
Willie Weasel, known to the underworld
as Willie the Weasel.'

I didn't like the look of him either.

'Top of the tree. Never loses a case.'

I was about to ask about *my* case but they were already half way out.

'How's the house coming on?' Sprog asked Willie.

'Am having the garden ripped up. For the swimming-pool. But the cost!'

'Don't tell me! You should see the bill for my jacuzzi and sauna!'

I was stunned. The only thing between me and a fate worse than death was this couple of money-eating sharks.

2 *The Daily Howl*

★ This newspaper can now reveal that
the trial of a well-known local criminal
begins next week. Mr Thomas Blake-
Burke Wolfe, aka The Big Bad Wolf, is
accused of Breaking and Entering the
house of Little Red Riding Hood's
grandmother with Intent to commit
Bodily Harm.

He is also charged with frightening
Miss Muffet and of Assaulting and

Injuring Mr Humpty Dumpty, a prominent figure in the community.

And on two counts of causing Criminal Damage to private property, namely, houses owned by two of the Three Little Pigs; and one count of Attempting to cause Criminal Damage to the house of the third.

It is widely believed that Mr TBB Wolfe may be further charged in connection with Bo Peep's sheep and an attempt on the lives of Jack and Jill. ★

3 The Trial Begins

The courtroom was packed to the gills
for the trial of the century. No
wonder. The whole thing had been the
talk of the village for weeks. Those
who couldn't get a seat hung out of
the ceiling and galleries. Those who
couldn't get in were at the windows.

Anyone who was anyone was there.

Old Mother Hubbard and Mother Goose sat in the front row. Jack Be Nimble and his brother Jack Be Quick were in the gallery. Georgie Porgie and his new girl-friend Mary, who was quite contrary, sat next to Jack and Jill.

Poor old Humpty Dumpty, still in plaster and on crutches, was given a special chair to protect him from the crush. Little Boy Blue and Bo Peep (minus her sheep who were turned away at the door) were there too.

Sprog looked sombre in a dark suit.
'For court...and funerals,' he winked.
The Weasel strolled in with a load of
papers. He waved to someone nearby.
'Hi, Sly,' he shouted. 'How's tricks?'

'That's Sylvester Fox,' said Sprog.
'For the Three Little Pigs. Well, mainly
for himself. Property. Worth millions.'
'Mr Weasel is a friend of Mr Fox's?
Isn't that unusual?'
'Lord, no. We're all friends – except
in court, of course.'
I had a lot to learn about the law.

'All rise,' said the White Rabbit, the
Court Clerk, as the judge took his seat.

'Well, shiver my timbers,' said
Sprog, 'if it isn't old Bill Boar. That's
a bit much.'

'Why?'

'Related to the Three Little Pigs.'

'Are you going to object?'

'Not worth it. Doesn't do to annoy
the judge before the trial starts.'

I looked at the jury who were mainly pigs and geese. Except one old sheep who had brought her knitting. She looked at me so intently I wondered if I had ever met her. Then I realised she was looking at my new sheepskin coat.

Had wearing it been a wise decision?

The charges were read: The Village versus Mr Thomas Blake-Burke Wolfe (known as The Big Bad Wolf), citing the cases of Red Riding Hood's grandmother, Little Miss Muffet, Humpty

16

Dumpty, and the Three Little Pigs.

First up was the crazy old grandma.

'Looks like an open and shut case to me,' barked Judge Bill Boar. 'Big bad wolf. In sheep's clothing! Poor little old lady. Alone. In fear of her life. Afraid. Where's the prisoner? Bring him up until I pass sentence.'

The coat had definitely been a no-no.

M'lud,' said The Weasel, 'there's just a teeny weeny matter to consider first.'

'What's that?' growled the judge.

'I think … I defer to your Lordship's superior judgment, of course … but I *think* we should have the trial first.'

'Trial? Sentence first, then the trial. That's how it used to be in the good old days. I don't hold with…' He paused as the White Rabbit whispered to him.

'Well, if you insist… Now, Mr

Weasel, does your client plead guilty?'

'Innocent as a new-born babe,' said
The Weasel. 'Denies everything.'

'Well he would, wouldn't he?'
smirked Sly.

'Call your first witness,' snapped the
judge to Sly, 'and don't be all day
about it. I have a lunch at 1 o'clock.'

'Known as "Necessity", sighed Sprog.
'Who?'

'The judge. Necessity knows no law.'
Sly rose to his feet.

'I call – Red Riding Hood's grandma!'

19

4 Grandma Comes a Cropper

It took quite a while to get grandma into the witness-box.

Then Sly said in honied tones, 'Now, tell the court, in your own words, just what happened the day The Big Bad Wolf broke in and attacked you.'

'I object,' said The Weasel, jumping to his feet. 'My learned friend is leading the witness. The facts have yet to be proved.'

'Oh, sit down, Mr Weasel,' said the judge. 'Everyone knows that The Big Bad Wolf broke into the old lady's house so he could eat her up.'

I was shocked to the core. How could I get a fair trial if the judge thought I was guilty? The jury would be swayed by him. Especially that pesky old sheep, who never took her eyes off my coat for a single instant.

'Well,' said Red Riding Hood's grandmother, ' I was all on my own, but I was expecting my grand-daughter to visit with some soup for me – I was in bed with a nasty cold. About lunch-time, that wolf fellow came in. I got an awful fright. He has a very bad reputation, you know. I had to throw things at him to get him out.'

'Thank you,' said Sly, bowing to the jury. 'I have no further questions.'

The Weasel got to his feet and shuffled his load of papers. He looked at the jury, then at the witness.

'Dear lady,' he said, 'how dreadful! Can you remember what happened just after you heard the knock on the door.'

A knock on the door! Did I knock? What if Sly asked me about it?

'Of course I can. I have a razor-sharp memory,' twittered the old lady. 'I thought it was Red Riding Hood with my lunch, so I called out "Come in."'

'And then what happened?'

'I saw it was The Big Bad Wolf.'

'Ah, what you are saying is that you *invited* Mr Wolfe into your house. Then you verbally abused him and threw things – including a frying-pan – at him.'

She was staring at him, mouth open.

'What I meant was…'

'You don't know *what* you meant – isn't that what you mean?' He turned to the jury. 'My client will testify that he heard she was ill and, out of the goodness of his heart, went to call on her. *With a bunch of flowers!* She invites him in, then assaults him.'

He turned to the old lady. 'You, with your razor-sharp memory, you saw the flowers, didn't you?' She nodded.

'That's all,' smirked The Weasel.

'Ignore that witness,' said the judge.

'That's the last of her and her razor-sharp memory,' sniggered Sprog to me.

Sly Fox rose. He had been going to object but what was there to object to?

'Call the woodcutter,' he said instead. He had been out-foxed!

The woodcutter, a fine burly man
with a bald head and a red hankie tied
around his neck, went into the witness-
box. He had his story off pat.

'I was working in the woods near
the house of Little Red Riding Hood's
grandmother, a dear lady and a great
friend, when one of the Three Little Pigs
came running up to say that The Big
Bad Wolf was attacking the old lady.'

'What did you do then?' asked Sly.

'I chased him away. I never saw anyone run so hard in my life.'

Big grin on his face, giving rise to 'laughter in court'. Judge Boar had to bang his hammer to restore order.

'So you chased my client with your axe. Is that correct?' asked The Weasel.

'Isn't that what I'm after saying.'

'At any time did you talk to him?'

'There wasn't time.'

'So, you actually didn't *see* my client do anything wrong, did you? But you didn't stop to ask any questions. You just chased him with an axe, shouting and using foul language, which,' looking at the jury, 'is unrepeatable here!

'It's a clear case of Intent to cause Grevious Bodily Harm. As for the Three Little Pigs ... they *incited* the woodcutter to Criminal Action.'

The court was stunned. The papers had said it was an open-and-shut case!

5 Miss M Turns Up Trumps

The judge looked stunned for a moment. Then he snapped, 'Next witness.'

This was Miss Muffet. She had flown into hysterics when a spider sat down beside her. I had no great hopes of her.

'No questions,' yawned Sly.

The Weasel took over. 'Now,' with a smile, 'what exactly happened outside Mr Humpty Dumpty's house? I don't have to remind a nice young lady like yourself to tell us the truth, the whole truth and nothing but the truth.'

Miss Muffet smiled back. 'I was just about to have my lunch when a big black spider dropped into my dish of whey and frightened the life out of me.'

'So it was the spider and *not* my client who frightened you, was it?'

'Yes. A great, big, black one.'

'Never mind the spider,' cut in Sly. 'Where was Mr Wolfe at this point?'

'He had just sat down beside me when the spider fell into my whey.'

'Then why did you tell the police that it was my client, Mr Wolfe, who frightened you?' asked The Weasel.

'I didn't. I told the police it was the spider but they said it was Mr Wolfe.'

Everyone gasped. Acting Chief of Police, Deputy Dodge, a cousin of the pig family, looked guilty as hell.

'But you *did* see Mr Wolfe push Mr Humpty Dumpty off the wall!' said Sly.

'Heavens, no!' replied Miss Muffet. 'I was too upset to see anything.'

Uproar! The open-and-shut case was in tatters. Reporters reached for their notebooks and their mobile phones.

Judge Bill Boar banged his hammer for all he was worth but it was useless.

The case had to be put off until the following day.

Everyone felt cheated. No more drama. No more shock surprises!

Frog & Sprog had won the day!

'What's the story?' yawned Snorer later.

'Good, I think. All the evidence given was disputed and Little Miss Muffet said the police were liars.'

'Better watch out,' said Croker. 'Old Sly won't take that lying down.'

'Time for the DTs,' said Wheezer.

'Dirty Tricks,' explained Croker. 'Bribing the jury. Nobbling witnesses.'

'Nobbling witnesses?'

'They disappear or they snuff it. Fall over cliffs. Get run down by a fast car.'

'Surely that would be a crime?'

'Boy, are you wet behind the ears. Old Sly wants to run for Mayor. Make the village safe for decent folk. He'll stop at nothing to put you behind bars. Better ring Sprog. Here's my mobile.'

A message flashed on: '*At Heebie-Jeebies gig. Only contact if you've murdered someone and not before ten.*'

'Nice lot of clients that guy has,' sneezed Wheezer.

6 More from *The Daily Howl*

Next morning *The Daily Howl* had it all.

SHOCKS IN COURT

★ What appeared to be an open-and-shut case against a well-known local underworld figure, Mr Thomas Blake-Burke Wolfe, seemed to collapse yesterday when the evidence of Red Riding Hood's grandmother and the wood-cutter was disputed and Little Miss Muffet said that the police had changed her statement.

Sources within the police say that she is known to be highly strung and it may be that she will be recalled when the Three Little Pigs give their side of the story today. They were also present when Mr Humpty Dumpty was pushed.

Mr Weasel, acting for Mr Wolfe, declined to comment. This newspaper believes that he is afraid of what the Three Little Pigs will say. Even a master of deception like The Weasel can hardly explain away the complete destruction of two houses. ★

7 Dirty Work at the Crossroads

I shall never forget day two of the trial as long as I live. The details are imprinted on my mind forever.

The day began normally enough. The usual breakfast of burnt porridge and sour milk. I pushed it aside.

There were cheers and jeers as I was led into the courtroom on that day.

The cheers were from the militant WPL (Wolf Protection League) who were taking a keen interest in my case.

The jeers were from the pig clan.

The jury still looked hostile – weren't they listening the day before? And that pesky old sheep kept staring at me even though I hadn't worn my sheepskin.

Sprog and The Weasel were in great form. I thought they both looked the worse for wear but I said nothing. I told them about Sly and the nobbling.

Howls of laughter. 'Well, if he nobbles, we'll gobble,' chortled Sprog.

'Be upstanding for his Honour, Judge Boar,' intoned the White Rabbit.

In came the judge who said to Sly, 'Call your first witness, don't dawdle.'

'I'm *recalling* a witness,' said Sly.

'Recalling? What for? All seemed clear-cut to me yesterday. Guilt of Mr Wolfe here obvious in spite of...'

The White Rabbit coughed.

'All right. All right. No need to get your tail in a twist about it. Just rehearsing my summing-up.'

I was stunned. The evidence of Red Hood's grandmother and the wood-cutter had been thrown out, and Little Miss Muffet had testified in my favour, but the judge hadn't changed his mind!

I turned to Sprog but he was polishing his nails. The Weasel, hands tucked into his waistcoat, was yawning.

I felt myself boiling over with rage. I could have killed either – or both.

'I recall,' said Sly, '*Little Miss Muffet.*'

There was a rustle of whispering.

What was the point in recalling *her*?

Then I relaxed. I could rely on her.

She was called again. No sign!

Another rustle of whispering.

'Where is she?' growled Judge Boar. 'I can't sit here all day waiting for her.'

He looked at the clock, then at his diary: *Posh Eaterie, 12.30 pm.*

'M'Lud,' said The Weasel, dragging himself to his feet, 'trick of my learned friend's. Delay the trial.'

'Fair point,' said the judge.

'We-need-Little-Miss-Muffet,' said Sly, pausing between every word, '*because of a dramatic new development.*'

More uproar in court!

'In the absence of Miss Muffet, I call Deputy Dodge, Acting Chief of Police.'

What *was* happening? Had I forgotten to take my big red pill that morning – the one that helps me to think clearly?

I was also feeling faint. Maybe I should have scraped away the burnt bits and forced down a little of the porridge.

Into the witness-box lumbered a small fat pig, a sheet of paper in his paw.

'M'Lud,' said Sly, 'I wish to have this document, which has just come to hand, admitted into evidence.'

'What is it?'

'A statement from Miss Muffet.'

Turning to Deputy Dodge, he went on, 'You took this statement?'

'Yup. That's the statement I tuk.'

'Please read it for the Court.'

Deputy Dodge took the paper and squinted at it.

'I, Miss Tuffet…Muffet…being of sound mind and of my own free will do here…hereby swear dat de Big Bad Wolf frighten…frightened me to debt.'

'I think the witness means "death",' said The Weasel smoothly. He and Sprog were in fits of laughing.

'...and also dat de said Big Bad Wolf
pushed poor Mr Dumpty off de wall.
Signed: Little Miss Buffet ... Muffet.'

'Are you sure it wasn't Stuffit?'
asked The Weasel keenly.

'Any more of that smart chit-chat,
Mr Weasel,' snarled the Judge, 'and
I'll have you banned from the Court.'

The Weasel struggled up again. He
had really been woeful today. Not at
all like yesterday. A touch of the
Heebie-Jeebies most likely.

'M'Lud,' he croaked hoarsely, 'surely you're not going to admit this so-called "statement". Where was it yesterday?'

'Good point, that,' said the Judge. 'Mr Sly, why wasn't it here yesterday?'

'The file went missing,' said Sly. 'That's what happens when our gallant police force is so overworked. They're working with a skeleton staff.'

'Not in this case!' said The Weasel.

Dodge, who must have weighed half a ton, turned even pinker than usual.

'So,' said the Judge to Sly, 'your witness certifies that Little Miss Muffet made this statement and signed it.'

'Yup,' said Dodge. 'And she said to me in her own words: "It was the Big Bad Wolf wot dun it. I seen it wid me own eyes."'

Surely the judge must see it was a forgery. Little Miss Muffet could never have written it. Or said '*dun*' it.

I was glad to see that he was looking anxious and making a few notes. (I found out, later, that he was changing his lunch date to 1 pm.)

'Where's Miss Muffet anyway,' he scowled. 'No sign of her yet? I'll put her in jail for Contempt of Court.'

'I've just had a message, m'Lud,' said Sly. 'She's disappeared! Gone without a trace. Leaving no address. Maybe the false evidence she gave yesterday preyed on her mind – as you know, she is an unstable character. That evidence is "unsafe" and should be thrown out.'

'I object,' said The Weasel, not even bothering to stand.

'My learned friend objects. To what?' Unsteady wave. 'Everything!'

'Unless she's here in five minutes,' snapped the judge, 'I'll take action.'

You could have heard a pin drop as the minutes ticked by. Five ... four ... three ... two ... one ....

'Enough!' roared the Judge. 'Jury, throw out the evidence Miss Muffet gave yesterday. The statement read b Deputy Dodge is allowed. Mr Sly, c your next witness.'

'Before we resume,' said Sly, 'I'm sure everyone here will want to offer sympathy to Little Red Riding Hood.'

'Why?' The judge looked irritated.

'Her grandmother was so upset by the antics of The Weasel that she had a complete breakdown last night. Lost her mind. We can only hope it comes back, slow though that process will be.'

'Not half as slow, I trust, as progress here,' scowled Judge Boar. 'Of course we're sorry, but get on with it, man.'

50

8 Uproar in Court!

At this stage my head was reeling. The case was turning upside down! With the Three Little Pigs to come, Humpty Dumpty was my only hope.

That is, if he was able to testify. His brain had been scrambled when he fell off the wall. Would Sly call him?

'I call ... Mr Humpty Dumpty!'

So he *was* to be called! My spirits rose. He would testify that the Three Little Pigs had caused his fall.

Looking very confused, he got up and hobbled over to the White Rabbit who directed him to the witness-box. But instead of going into it, he went up to the Judge's bench and tried to sit beside the judge.

'Mr Dumpty,' said Judge Boar sternly, 'do you know where you are?'

'Yes, of course, Vicar. But I can't seem to find my prayer-book.'

He was directed once more to the witness-box but as he came down the steps, *I saw Sly, who was standing nearby, put out his stick and trip him up*!

There was a terrible crash as poor old Humpty tumbled down. His head looked in bits. Was he dead?

I need hardly say there was uproar. Doctors and nurses were called. Heart machines rolled in. Humpty was loaded on to a stretcher and taken away.

In the midst of all this, old Judge Boar vanished, calling out as he went, 'Court resumes – three o'clock sharp!'

Shortly after three o'clock, Judge Bill
Boar bounded back, licking his lips, a
silly smile on his face.

'Next witness, Mr Sly,' he slurred.

'I call the Three Little Pigs.'

I closed my eyes. I was for it!

One by one, they tripped into the
witness-box. Each told exactly the same
story about how they had seen the Big
Bad Wolf attack Red Riding Hood's

grandmother, frighten Miss Muffet almost to death, push Humpty Dumpty off the wall, and, finally, attack them in their own homes. Two of them said he had huffed and puffed and blown their houses down and would have eaten them up if they had not escaped to their eldest brother's house – the brick one.

'We were lucky,' they said, tears in their eyes. 'We would have been killed only The Big Bad Wolf is getting slow on his feet. He can't run any more.'

The eldest brother described how The Big Bad Wolf had done his best to demolish his house too, before being knocked senseless by a falling slate.

There was hardly a dry eye in the Court when the three had finished.

'My case – the Village against The Big Bad Wolf – rests,' said Sly.

The Weasel dragged himself up. He and Sprog looked worse than ever.

But just at that moment, Judge Boar half rose in his seat. He clutched his heart, gave a moan, then slowly subsided behind the bench.

He did not get up.

The uproar after Humpty Dumpty's collapse was nothing to this. The place was swarming with doctors and nurses and heart machines. The police poured in and arrested everyone in sight. Reporters rushed around with mikes and mobiles and TV cameras.

Finally the word came through.

Judge Bill Boar was dead.

9 *The Daily Howl* Sums up.

★ 'Your reporter can reveal that never in all his years can he recall scenes like those enacted in the courthouse yesterday. Apart from the shocks of the trial itself – see pages two, three, four, five and six – we had the collapse

of Mr Humpty Dumpty. His condition is still unknown.

Then came the tragic event that has shaken the Village to the core, the death of Judge Bill Boar, struck down in the prime of life as he was handling this very difficult and important case in his usual fair and impartial way. Our sympathy lies with his stricken family. His funeral, which will be in two days' time, is bound to be one of the largest ever seen in the Village.

Meanwhile, your Reporter can bring you up to date on the where-abouts of some of the most important people in this great drama which has been unfolding before our eyes.

When Judge Boar was declared dead, Mr Thomas Blake-Burke Wolfe, aka The Big Bad Wolf, was whisked away by the WPL (Wolf Protection League). It is not known where he is at present. Bail has been applied for.

Little Miss Muffet seems to have disappeared into thin air. The police have listed her as 'Missing'.

Red Riding Hood's grandmother is still in hospital. No visitors are allowed.

No date for the retrial has been set. ★

Footnote by Mr TBB Wolfe: 'Did you know that wolves and foxes belong to the same family? That's why I found it odd that Sly Fox was on the opposite side. No clan loyalty!

It's easy to tell us apart, by the way. He's the one with the *pointed* ears.

PS: Look out for my next book, *The Retrial of the Big Bad Wolf.* Details later.

A little about Elephants

If you had to write 'A Day in the Life of an Elephant' what would you write?

It should go something like this:

Dawn: Up at the crack of. Take a gentle stroll, eating all along the way.

Noon: Rest under the trees.

Afternoon: Feed. Bathe if there is any water around.

Evening: More walking, more eating.

Night: Sleep. Maybe the odd little snack.

There's a lot of eating, isn't there?

Someone worked out we eat for about nineteen out of every twenty-four hours!

A Little about Reading

 The trouble with a book
about anything to do
with the law is all the
long words they use.

They never use a short word when
they can use a long one. Preferably a
very long one. And they string them
all together. Very off-putting.

But don't panic!

Remember what I told you about
breaking up words.

When you see long words like
'Breaking and Entering', 'Assaulting
and Injuring'. 'Bribing and Nobbling',
see if you can break them up.

You can – just lop off the 'ing'.

That cuts them down to size!

Works for non-legal words too.

Elephants – easy reading for new readers who have moved on a stage. Still with –
   Large type
   Mostly short words
   Short sentences
   Lots of illustrations
   And fun!

There are now three **Elephants**:
1. *The True Story of the Three Little Pigs and the Big Bad Wolf*
2. *The Hungry Horse*
3. *The Trial of the Big Bad Wolf*

Liam Farrell lives in Maynooth, Co Kildare. He has one daughter, Lydia, a son, Jeremy, and three grandsons, Garrett, Braiden and Liam.
   He has now written two 'Wolf' books and a third, *The Retrial of the Big Bad Wolf* is on the way.

Terry Myler, one of Ireland's best-known illustrators, has also written *Drawing Made Easy* and *Drawing Made Very Easy*.